I'm Reading About

WISCONSIN

The Badger State!

GALLOPADE

by Carole Marsh

Printed and Manufactured in Peachtree City, GA., USA
www.gallopade.com

Book design: John Hanson

Editorial manager: Janice Baker

Wisconsin is a great state.

It is one of a kind.

What makes Wisconsin special?

Let's read about it

and see!

NATIVE AMERICANS

Who lived in Wisconsin first?

Native Americans did!

They moved around to find food.
They hunted in Wisconsin's woods.
They fished in Wisconsin's rivers.
They gathered fruits and seeds and nuts.

EXPLORERS

The first explorers came to Wisconsin in 1634.
They came from the country of France.

Jean Nicolet was their leader.
He and his men were looking for a route
to the Pacific Ocean!

SETTLEMENT

Father Claude Allouez came from France to America. He built one of the first missions in Wisconsin. He built it at Green Bay.

A mission was a place built to bring the Christian religion to the native people.

Green Bay
Green Bay
EAST RIVER

STATEHOOD

Wisconsin was the 30th state
to join the United States of America!

Isn't it great,
to be a state!
I bet Wisconsin
could hardly wait!

Wisconsin became a state in 1848.

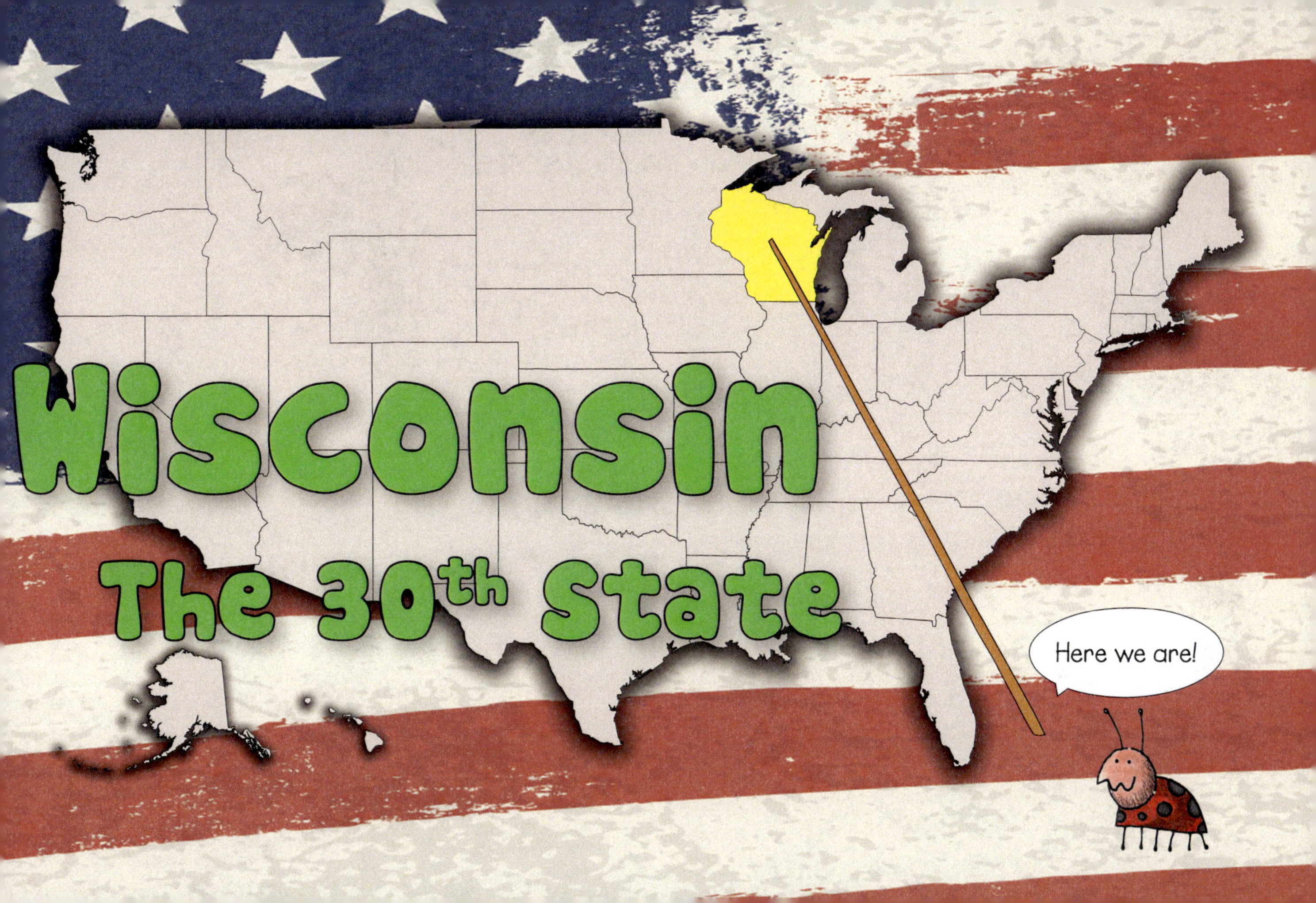
Wisconsin
The 30th State
Here we are!

FLAG

I am the state flag.

What color am I?
I am blue.

Look at me.
What else do you see?

I fly high over the state of Wisconsin!

WISCONSIN
FORWARD
E PLURIBUS UNUM
1848

CAPITAL

Say hello to Madison,
the capital city of Wisconsin!

There is an important building in Madison.
It is the State Capitol.
Wisconsin's laws are made there!

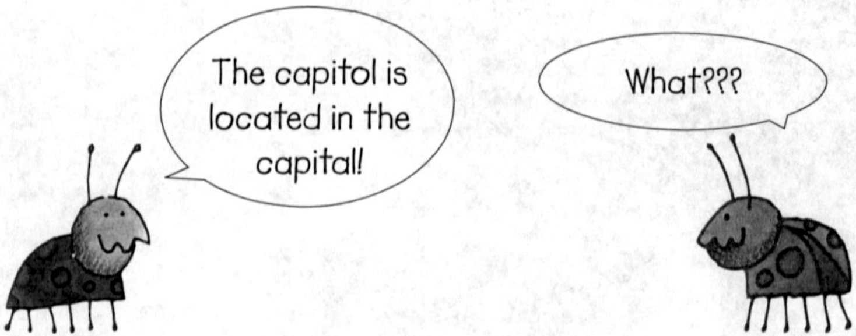

Capitol
Madison
Capital

SEAL

I am a seal,
but I am not the State Seal.
If I were, I would be very important.
I would be stamped on many official papers.
(Ouch, that might hurt!)

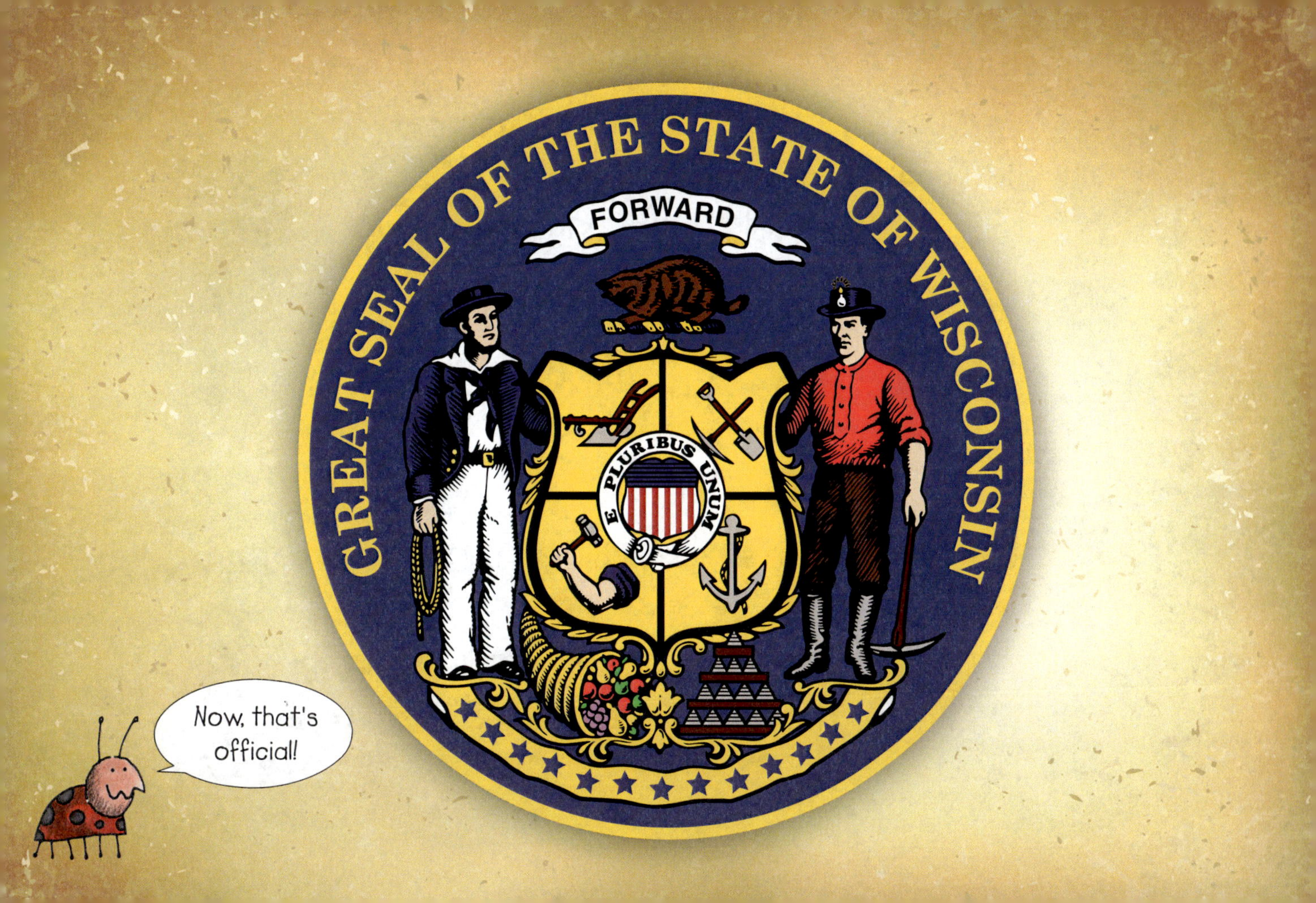
GREAT SEAL OF THE STATE OF WISCONSIN
FORWARD
E PLURIBUS UNUM
Now, that's official!

NICKNAME

State nicknames are fun!
State nicknames are great!
They share fun facts
about each state!

Wisconsin's nickname is "The Badger State."

Badgers have long claws to dig in the dirt!
They live underground in burrows.

The Badger State

BORDERS

Look at Wisconsin.
Wisconsin is in a region called "the Midwest."

Wisconsin borders four other states.
Find them on the map!

Wisconsin comes from an Indian word that means "grassy place."

Borders

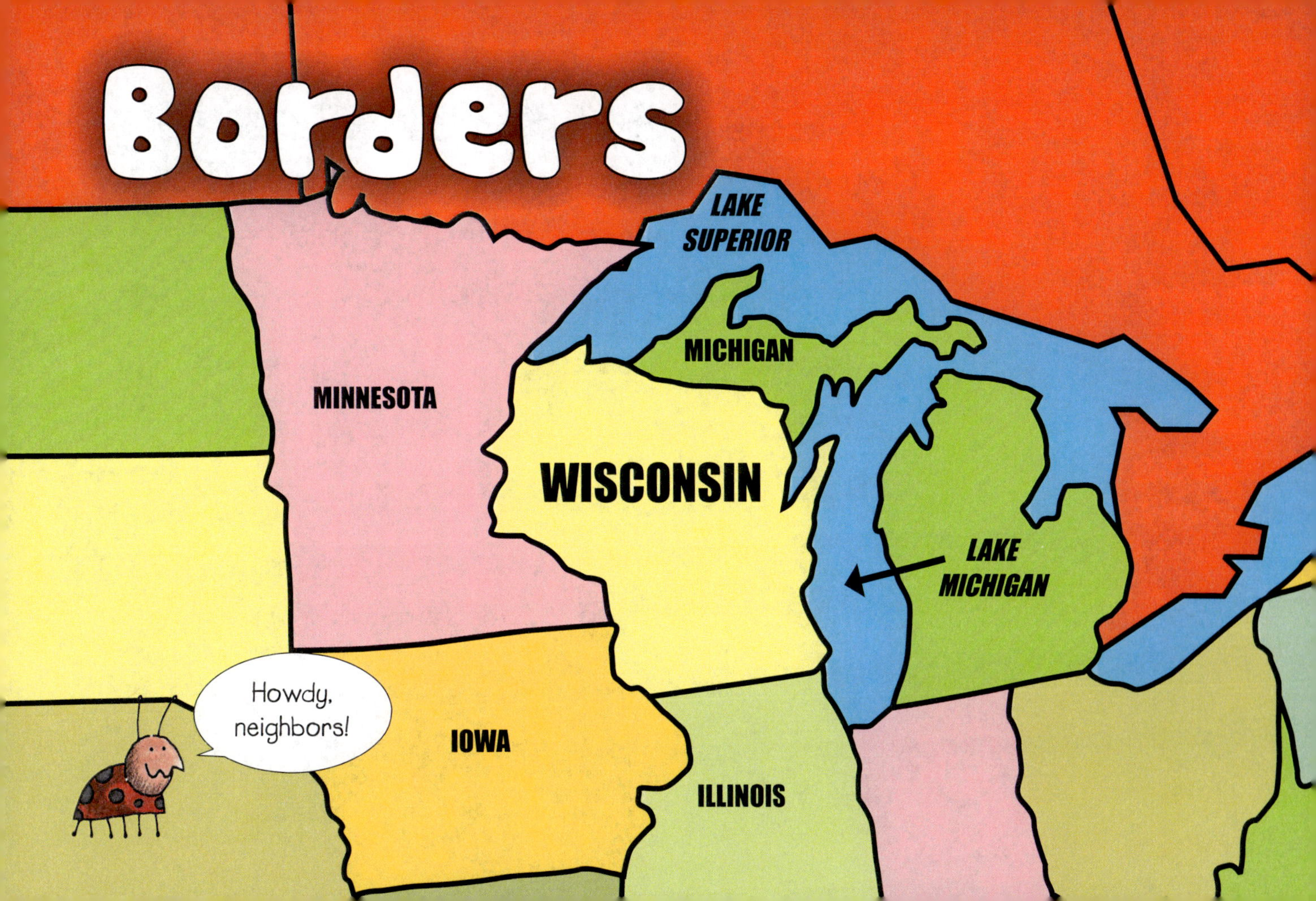
LAKE SUPERIOR
MICHIGAN
MINNESOTA
WISCONSIN
LAKE MICHIGAN
Howdy, neighbors!
IOWA
ILLINOIS

COUNTIES

Wisconsin is divided into 72 counties.
Counties are a form of local government.
Counties provide services that people need!
Those services include:

Schools **Parks** **Libraries**

Police **Firefighters** **and More!**

Counties

WISCONSIN'S CAPITAL, MADISON, IS IN DANE COUNTY.

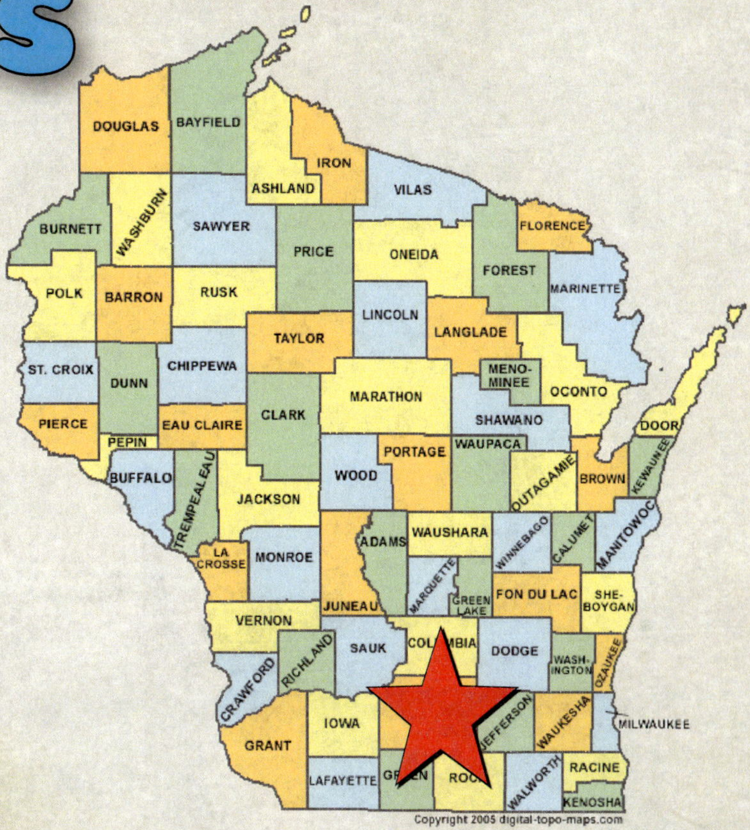

PEOPLE

Many famous people

King C. Gillette

Invented a safety razor that changed the shaving industry

Ringling Brothers

Creators of the Ringling Brothers Circus

Laura Ingalls Wilder

Author of Little House on the Prairie

call our state home!

PEOPLE

Frank Lloyd Wright

Known as one of the greatest architects of the 20th century

Harry Houdini

Magician and escape artist

Eric Heiden

Speed skater who won five Olympic gold medals

Robin

BIRD

I am the state bird, and I fly
over Wisconsin, proud and high.

As I fly, up in the sky,
I flap my wings to tell you "Hi!"

The Wisconsin state bird is the Robin.

Wood Violet

FLOWER

I am the Wood Violet.
I am the state flower.

I grow where it's warm and sunny.
I bloom in spring and summer.
I help make Wisconsin beautiful!

Look at me! Smell me!
People make tasty jelly
from my blooms!

Sugar Maple

TREE

I am a Sugar Maple—I'm the state tree.
All over Wisconsin is where to find me.

My roots run deep, they keep me strong.
I can live for hundreds of years—that's very long!

I stand up straight, big and tall.
Don't climb too high—it would hurt to fall!

Honeybee

INSECT

I am the Honeybee.
I am the state insect.

I might sting you if you bother me,
But really, I am your friend.

I carry pollen from flower to flower.
I make honey.
I help Wisconsin crops grow.

BZZZZZZZZZZZZ!

Lakes

LAKES

Let's go to the lake!

We can wade in the water.
We can ride on a boat.

We can jump off the dock
onto an inner tube float!

Lake Michigan and Lake Superior
are home to many animals:

Fish **Snakes** **Birds** **Turtles** **Salamanders** **and More!**

Northern Highlands

HIGHLANDS

Wisconsin's Northern Highlands are the place to be.
Hiking, fishing, camping—
fun for you and me.

Winter weather brings lots of snow!
Temperatures drop to freezing and below.

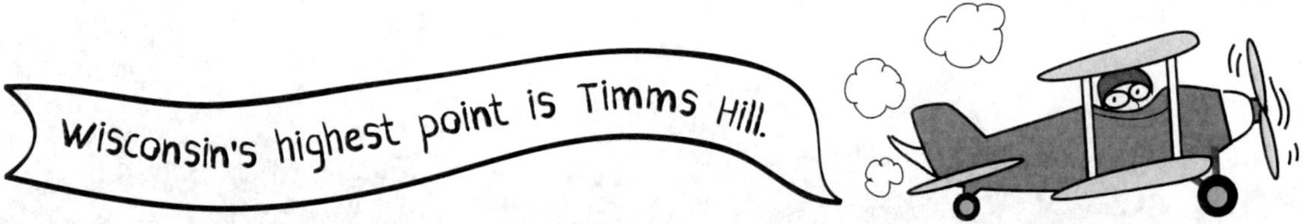

Rivers

RIVERS

Wisconsin has many rivers.
People like to use them for boating and fishing!

This habitat is home to many animals:

Birds Deer Snakes Frogs Fish and More!

Rivers were Wisconsin's first highways.
People floated down
the rivers on flatboats.
They carried goods to sell or trade.

Apostle Islands

LANDMARK

The Apostle Islands are located along the northern tip of Wisconsin.
They are in Lake Superior.

Visitors to the Apostle Islands can see:

Rock Formations **Sea Caves** **Lighthouses**

Shipwrecks **and More!**

Wisconsin Crops

AGRICULTURE

Wisconsin has many farms.
Why?
Because Wisconsin has good soil and a mild climate!

Some of the top crops grown in Wisconsin are:

Corn **Soybeans** **Potatoes** **Cranberries**

Sports in Wisconsin

SPORTS

Baseball! Basketball! Football! Hockey!
Wisconsin has it all.

Whether you like to watch or play,
You are sure to have a ball!

Brewers **Bucks** **Packers**

Badgers

Panthers

Golden Eagles **& More!**

Wisconsin: Home of Cheese

Wisconsin is known for its cheese!
Wisconsin makes the most cheese in America.

Many other dairy products come from Wisconsin, too.
Dairy products include milk, butter, and cheese.

People from Wisconsin are sometimes called "cheeseheads"!

GLOSSARY

architect: a person who designs buildings

burrow: a hole or tunnel dug by an animal for it to live in

climate: weather conditions in an area over a long period of time

dairy product: a food item containing milk or made from milk

habitat: a place where plants or animals naturally live

laws: rules made by the government

pollen: a yellow powder that helps plants make new plants

region: an area that has similar characteristics

safety razor: a razor with a guard to reduce the risk of cutting the skin

settlement: the first community in an area